I0699888

Working Blue Press

First Edition

ISBN 978-1-967038-05-3 (Kindle)
ISBN 978-1-967038-06-0 (Print)

For all the women who love good sex,
and all the meals you've eaten while
talking about it with good friends.

Content

Suggestions for Further Reading

Girls Who Brunch Erotic Series
Books 1, 2, 3 and 4.

Follow Lacey Love on Amazon to keep abreast of new releases!

Extra Whipped Cream

Girls Who Brunch Erotic Series

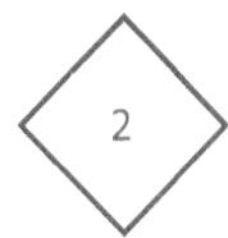

1

Extra Whipped Cream

"Ace." Summer slid into the standard wood chair of the mom and pop's diner on the East side of Cleveland and dropped her Chanel purse down on to the floor as her long, black hair swayed and glistened. She pulled her black, wraparound-sunglasses off and took a deep breath as she quietly placed them on the square, simple table and smiled.

Her three besties from her days at Ohio State readjusted in their seats, as they glanced between each other with surprise and then at her.

"Ace?" Annie repeated. Summer flicked a stare at the green-eyed blonde who was sporting a mischievous grin.

"In the hole?" Fawn asked as she chuckled.

"Which hole?" Tabitha chimed in with a laugh as she put down her gin and juice.

Annie spit a little mimosa out as she chuckled.

"I kid," Tabitha said. "But not really. So, what? Ace…up your sleeve?"

Annie quickly followed up. "Or maybe, aces." She used a surfer's tone and body language as she smiled jokingly.

"Hilarious, assholes," Summer said sarcastically as the waiter sauntered up.

"Morning," he said with a sexy lilt to his voice.

"No, to that," Summer said. She waved her thin fingers at his round, pimpled face. "But yes, to a vodka and pineapple juice. Heavy on the vodka."

The waiter turned down his hazel eyes at her quick rejection but recovered quickly. "Right away."

As he slinked off, Summer smoothed down her dark, brown leather tights and cream-colored, cashmere sleeveless shirt. She let out a breath and looked at three pairs of questioning eyes.

"So," Annie prodded. "Anything you wanna tell us?"

"No." Summer crossed her arms over her chest with a grin. "How's your throuple?"

"Delicious." Annie flung her long, blonde curls over her shoulder as her breasts jiggled happily in the expensive, white tank top she was wearing with simple blue jeans. The diamond necklace made from Tommy's ring sparkled on her chest. "But this isn't about me and my two hot men. You texted all of us to have an emergency brunch, then you sit yourself down and say 'Ace,' and now nothing?"

"I call bullshit." Tabitha shot Summer a suspicious look with her icy, blue eyes and topped it off with a haughty eyebrow raise. Tabitha was sporting an auburn should-length bob today, and a natural make-up pallet. Her plus-sized figured was wrapped in a seductive palm-leaf print summer dress. *Love that she always has a new look.*

"Come on, Summer," Fawn said sweetly. Summer noticed that Fawn's normally dishwater-blonde hair had platinum blonde streaks in them now and her racy, little spaghetti-strap shirt with no bra was more salacious than usual. "Your text said otherwise. So…spill."

"It started when he told me his name was Ace," Summer said as she leaned forward.

"Oooooo," Tabitha squealed as she twiddled her fingers in excitement.

"Now, this is brunch talk," said Annie. She readjusted her slim body to face Summer as she propped her elbow on the back of her chair and leaned her head into her hand. "So, Ace is a 'he'?"

"A very, very hot 'he'," Summer said. She rubbed her face before dropping her head into her own hands.

"And one you seem to like," Fawn said. At that, they all leaned toward her.

"Fuck me." Summer slapped the table and slammed back into her chair with a joyful thud.

"Ohhhh!" Tabitha said, as the other two girls equaled her enthusiasm.

"Summer likes a guy!" Annie's grin was barely contained by her cheeks.

"I never thought I'd see the day." Fawn grabbed her coffee and took a sip.

"So, what happened?" Annie asked.

The waiter returned and placed Summer's drink in front of her. "Ready to order?"

"Yes," Summer said. "I'm starving. I'll take a pile of French toast—"

"With whipped cream?" The waiter asked.

"Extra whipped cream," Summer said. She peered at the girls with a grin and said quietly. "That's the second time I've said that in as many days."

"Oh shit," Tabitha squealed. "This is gonna be good."

"You have no idea." Summer smiled as she started to talk.

2

Call Me Ace

Summer would never forget the first time she spoke to him.

"You can call me Ace," he had said smoothly. They were in a "key-entry only" high-end bar on the west side of Cleveland, where high rollers came to spend thousands a night on one glass of alcohol that cost more than her monthly mortgage.

"You can call me anytime," she'd flirted back as his large, strong hand had gripped hers in a flirtatious shake. It was accompanied by a sultry stare from his bright hazel eyes that were lit with humor.

He had looked down at her from the three extra inches of height he had over her, even with her wearing two-inch heels, and smiled. His perfect, pearly-white teeth gleamed from his wide grin.

Summer should have known in that moment that Ace was a nickname and to ask for his real name but, holy shit, he was the hottest, older man she'd ever seen.

His hair was dark with just a touch of gray, and wavy and short with just enough length for her small hands to grip. His full lips twitched up in a smile at her boldness.

At first, she didn't want to know anything about him except what it felt like to have him between her legs. She was celebrating, dammit. And after a couple glasses of champagne, she was ready to take him to bed and show him what it felt like to slide in and out of a woman who just closed a multi-million-dollar deal.

"Why call when I can take you home with me right now?" he'd asked smoothly. A jolt of electricity had shot through her body when he had said it, and it only took a few minutes for them to agree that was a bad idea.

She was all for women having the right to a one-night stand just like men, but she also didn't want to end up the subject of a streaming service's true crime episode, either.

"Funny," he'd laughed when she'd said that out loud. "And true. I respect that."

His eyes had glittered with attraction as he had told her about a VIP room in the back where they could have more privacy.

"I have a key," he'd offered. "And, for your safety, you can tell the bartender where you're at and to check on you in an hour. I'll even leave my driver's license with him if that will make you feel better, too."

It had. And so that's exactly what she had done, though she'd asked for two hours, of course. She was pretty sure that move to keep her safe was what allowed them to have such great sex in the VIP room of the plushest club in Cleveland.

"More!" She had screamed so loud she swore someone might come in, but if anyone heard, they just let them have their have fun. And boy, was it fun.

"Fuck, you're amazing," he had yelled as he thrust his throbbing cock deep inside her over and over again. She'd never been so wet in her life. When they had got in the room, he'd slowly slid her black, leather dress off her body, but left her strappy heels on. He'd lifted her onto the bar, then sat between her legs and licked her pussy like it was an ice cream cone.

"You taste amazing," he had said. He'd grabbed her thighs and spread her wide open as his tongue slid up and down her lips, pausing to suck on her clit before driving it deep into her pussy.

"God, yes!" She'd grabbed his hair then and moved his head in time with her pulsing hips. She had watched him eat her with delight, moaning as he brought her to the edge of her orgasm before stopping and dropping his dark blue jeans revealing he was going commando. His throbbing, thick cock was a welcome sight. "Slide it in me!"

He'd picked her up from the bar and dropped them both on the leather couch in the VIP lounge and slid that beast inside her as she moaned with pleasure.

"Ace, yes!" And then he'd fucked her. Fucked her so good,

she didn't want to stop. But two minutes after she came, the loyal bartender, true to his word, knocked on the door.

They'd both quickly gotten dressed and opened the door with a smile as the bartender handed Ace his driver's license back.

"Thank you," Ace had said.

"Yes," she said. "Thank you."

As she went to leave, Ace had grabbed her gently by the waist to stop her. When she had turned to face him, he had said, "I know this was for fun, but—"

"That's right," she had interrupted. "It was just for fun."

And then a moment had passed between them and as she gazed into his eyes, she had felt something else.

"I mean," she started as she gazed at him. She had suddenly wanted to take back her quick words as warmth came back to her from his eyes. As she started to change her mind, her coworkers had appeared.

"Summer!" they had yelled.

They had run up to her and grabbed her. "We're headed to Sam's to continue the party. Let's go!"

As they had pulled her out of the bar, she locked eyes with him one more time and he smiled with a nod.

She cursed herself the next morning as she thought about Ace and why she hadn't just listened to him and gotten his number.

Wait, what am I doing? It was just a one-night stand. I don't do relationships. Not right now anyway. Not yet.

She was at the prime of her career and she wanted to invest her time in building it before having outside interruptions. This latest deal that she had been celebrating

was going to set her up in a big
way. The money was going to fund
her retirement, buy her a new car,
and finally allow her to get that
teeny-tiny vacation house on the
beach in Top Sail, North Carolina.

Top Sail was where her family
had vacationed when she was a
child and it held wonderful
memories for her and her brothers.
After their parents died in a car
accident, Summer and her brothers
stopped going. But now, she felt it
was time to go back. And this little
house was her way back to those
warm days on the beach with her
mother and father.

She touched a framed photo of
her parents on her cool, sleek
fireplace. Her whole place was
decorated in a contemporary look
and feel and furnished in clean
whites, creams, silvers and blacks.
But her love of nature gave way to
the overabundance of big green

plans, potted flowers, and a couple small trees in colorful pots.

She nodded her approval at the clean design then curled up on her plush couch and wrapped her chunky blanket around her. *Maybe I'll see him again at the bar. We go there a lot to celebrate.*

She took a couple aspirins after last night's celebration and curled up for a weekend nap. And maybe, just maybe, she'd have a sexy little dream about Ace.

~~~

By Monday morning, Summer felt great about her weekend. She'd won a huge contract, had great sex, and put in an offer for the Top Sail beach house. She strolled into her company wearing her red stiletto heels and black Vera Wang leather
~~~

dress as she sashayed into her office. Her coworker, Dustin, followed her through the door as she walked to her desk.

She sat down as he said, "Ready to meet the new CEO?"

"Oh yeah," she said. She flipped open her laptop and started scrolling through her emails. "I forgot that was today. Meet and greet, right? And he officially takes over next Monday?"

"Yep," Dustin said. "I hear he's very cool. Good, too."

"Awesome," she said.

"Congrats again on your big contract," he said. "You still feelin' good? Minus the Saturday hangover, of course."

She laughed. "Right? I'm getting too old for that anymore. Almost thirty."

"Almost," he said. "But you still look twenty."

"What do you want?" she asked suspiciously of his generous comment.

"Nothin', I swear," he said. "Except a good word with the new CEO when he starts."

"What makes you think he'd listen to me about anything?"

"Come on," he said. "You're the top salesperson here. You'll be in the inner circle. Especially if you get the promotion to VP of Sales."

She let out a big sigh. "God, I want that."

"Oh you've got it. There's no competition. You earned it." He checked his watch. "Doh, we better go."

"Oh, right," she said. She grabbed her coffee and followed him out of the office to the conference room. As she sat down, thoughts of Ace drifted into her mind. *He was so cute. And so good in bed.*

Everyone got seated including her boss, Dalia, the president of Sales and Marketing. Dalia would be the one to promote her, which made Summer happy. Dalia was her boss, but also a friend and confidant.

"Good weekend?" Dalia asked with a smile.

"Excellent," Summer said.

"You deserved it," Dalia quipped. She got the teleconference video ready as the team hustled in with coffees and pastries. "Alright, everyone, gather around. The new CEO is going to be incredible. You're all gonna love him. So let's meet him."

As they all focused on the screen, Summer took a sip of her black coffee, one sweetener. Just as the hot liquid reached her mouth, she quickly spit it out, hitting Dustin with it.

"Whoa," he said. He leaned away from her and wiped himself off as Dalia kept cool and ignored it. She glanced at the screen with the new CEO smiling back at all of them.

"Good to see you again, Mr. Black," said Dalia. "Everyone, this is Micah Black, our new CEO."

Summer wiped her mouth and clothes as she took in the man on the screen.

Holy shit.

Ace.

3

The Proposal

Summer glanced around her office and realized it was now past dinner time and she had spent the day hiding behind her computer screen and not answering anyone when they asked why.

I can't believe Ace—or rather, Micha Black—is the new CEO.

When she had seen him on the screen, she couldn't stop the coffee from spewing out of her mouth. As he spoke to her team, eloquently and with genuine passion for the work, all she could think about was how his hard cock had driven into her repeatedly Friday night, making her come three times in two hours.

"Ugh," she groaned. She rubbed her face and leaned back in her chair with a sigh. Being near him was going to be difficult. She already knew she'd want him. She wanted him right now. Even though he was now, apparently, her boss.

As her stomach grumbled at her, she realized she hadn't eaten today, and she was starving. She quickly wrapped up the last of her sales reports and hit send. Dalia would be pleased at the numbers, and it would elevate Summer to the top of the list for the VP of Sales promotion.

"Thanks, Dalia, goodnight," a male voice said down the hall, followed by heavy footsteps and then the soft click of the restroom door. Right after that she heard another set of footsteps in the hallway clicked toward her.

"Got your report," Dalia said as she leaned into Summer's office. "Now go home. Great job."

"Okay, thanks, Dalia," Summer replied.

"So, what was the coffee thing about today?"

"Oh, that." Summer hesitated. "Nothing. Just…coffee was hot and it surprised me."

"That's it?"

"That's it."

"Okay," Dalia said suspiciously. "Well, have a good night then."

"You, too." Summer listened as Dalia clicked down the hallway, grabbed her things from her office, and left. A few seconds later, she heard the soft click of the restroom door again and the heavy footsteps from before walking toward her door.

Who could that possibly be?

She leaned forward in her seat as the footsteps approached. She gasped when the familiar face peered around the doorframe.

"Hey there," Ace said with a wide grin.

She leaned back in her chair as a surprised breath escaped her throat. "Ace Black."

"Summer Spring." He stepped inside her door. "Do people ever note the irony in your name?"

"All the time." She shifted her hips as she felt the blood flow to her most intimate places. The thought of his cock inside her made her pussy start to ache. "You look good."

And he did. His sleek black Tom Ford suit was fit perfectly against his sculpted body and his hair was perfectly styled. She wanted to unbutton his shirt with her teeth and pull out his thick cock.

"You look gorgeous," he said. His eyes shifted to her heels as his gaze slid up her legs to her face. "So, I guess starting Monday I'm your new boss. Surprised?"

"You have no idea," she said. She turned her chair toward him and slid her legs silkily against each other, opening them just wide enough to catch his stare. "Did you know?"

He shook his head. "No idea until I saw you in that room."

"You didn't show it." She smiled seductively.

"Trust me," he said as he eyed her legs that she was brazenly showing him. "I felt it. Why do you think I'm here now?"

"What do you mean?" she asked.

"I had no need to come down here today," he said. "I made up a reason. I wanted to see you."

A fiery heat started to form in her gut and spread through her body. So, he wanted to see her, too. And now here they were. Alone. In her office.

"You know, I'm not officially your boss for seven more days," he said. He took a step closer. "And while, having a relationship after

next Monday would be a bad idea,
there's nothing stopping us from
enjoy the time until then."

"Oh yeah?" she asked.

"Yeah," he said. He stepped
further into her office. As he
walked toward her, she could see
his cock straining against the
expensive fabric.

"What do you have in mind?"

"A proposal," he said.

"I won't marry you this fast,"
she joked.

He laughed. "Clever," he said.
He kept moving closer like a
panther on the hunt. "The proposal
is that you take a week off after
your big win, starting now, and join
me at my lake cabin for…some
relaxation."

He closed the distance between
them.

"And what kind of…relaxation
did you have in mind?" She
uncrossed her legs and spread them

slightly as he came and stood between them.

"I'm glad you asked."

He reached down and slid his fingers between her legs as she moaned.

"Yes," she said.

She gripped his shoulders as he kissed her deeply and thrust his fingers into her.

"God, you're wet," he moaned.

She reached over and unbuckled his belt, unzipping him and stroking his hard cock.

"Yes," he moaned.

He pulled his fingers out and lifted her off the chair onto the desk.

"Fuck yes," she said.

He yanked her dress up her thighs and dropped to his knees as he spread her legs and dipped his tongue into her slit, eating and licking her with wild abandon.

"Fuck, yes!" She writhed with pleasure as he moaned. "Take me now."

He stood and slid her off the desk, turning her around and bending her over the glass top as her pens and pencils spilled onto the floor.

"Fuck me, Ace!" She moaned as he pulled her dress completely over her hips and sunk his cock deep inside her. "Oh, fuck me!"

And he did. He pounded his cock into her soaking wet pussy as his hands slid under her dress and up her smooth stomach. He grabbed hold of her soft, pillowy breasts, twisting her nipples with his fingers.

"Harder," she yelled. "Fuck me harder."

"Summer, fuck!" he moaned. He pounded her harder as her hips banged against the desk.

"I'm gonna come!" she howled with pleasure.

"I'm coming, too," he yelled.

She came hard as he pulled out and came on her back. She could barely handle how good the warm, salty fluid felt as it landed on her warm skin at the same her orgasm peaked.

As they both finished and started to relax into the afterglow, he grabbed a tissue from her desk and cleaned her up. He helped her stand as he straightened her dress and gave her a smile.

"I didn't come here for that," he said. He started picking up the pens and pencils from the floor. "But I'm glad it happened."

"Me too," she said.

"So, about the cabin," he said. He placed the remaining items from the floor back on her desk, then shoved his hands in his pockets. "I think it could be fun."

"Me too," she said. She smoothed down her hair. "But I'd like to think about it overnight. You are going to be my boss, after all. Something to consider."

"That's fair," he said. "If you'd like to join me, text me your address." He grabbed one of the pens and jotted his number down on a piece of scrap paper. He slid it toward her. "I'll be outside your house at 7 a.m. to pick you up if you do. I'll wait five minutes. If you come, great. If you don't, I understand. And I'll see you on Monday."

"Okay," she said. "I appreciate that."

She really did appreciate that he always considered her feelings and what would make her feel safe, giving her time and space to make her decision.

"No problem," he said. He lightly kissed her on the cheek. "I hope I see you in the morning."

She sighed as she watched him walk out, taking in the smell of his cologne and how his presence always made her feel at ease. She gathered her things to leave. She had a lot to think about.

And she was glad Ace was at the top of that list.

4

Hands All Over Me

As the warm water flowed over her body in the shower, Summer took a deep breath. It was closing in on 7 a.m. and she was still deciding about whether or not she was going to go.

Oh stop, you already decided. The email to Dalia at midnight had said as much: "Hi Dalia, I'm taking some much-needed vacation time, hope it's okay, blah, blah, blah."

She wanted to go, there was no doubt. The issue was him being her boss. It was sexy, of course. He was sexy, of course. But how many workplace romances with the boss ever ended well for the woman? Especially one with career sites set as high as hers?

This is a bad idea.

She reached between her legs and massaged her clit as it throbbed. Just thinking about him made her squirm. Her other hand reached up and massaged her nipples, squeezing them and twisting them as she gasped with pleasure. The warm water ran between her legs as she quickened the pace against her clit, squeezing her nipples harder.

"Yes," she moaned. She rubbed her clit faster and faster and squeezed her nipples harder. "Yes!"

She felt her orgasm rush through her body as she imagined Ace's tongue in her slit. "Oh, yes," she said as she came harder and harder. "Fuck."

She was breathless as the water massaged her skin with a light pressure. She quickly jumped out of the shower, grabbed a towel and

dried off, then texted him her
address.

Bad idea or not—and it *was* a
bad idea—she was going.

~~~

Ace wasn't sure why he wanted
Summer so badly.

He'd had plenty of one-night
stands with beautiful younger
women just like her. She was
maybe eight or nine years his junior
with gorgeous brown eyes and jet-
black hair that brushed against her
breasts. She was always dressed
impeccably, and her intelligence
oozed from every pore in her body.

She was successful, beautiful,
and funny. And when he was with
her, he felt…different.

*Shake it off. You can't go down
this path.*
~~~

She was, ultimately, going to be his employee. And he had never in his whole career crossed that line. It never worked for either party involved, and he always kept business and pleasure separate from each other. And with Summer, he wouldn't want to ruin her career, or his.

But I don't think I can stay away from her, either.

Maybe this week with her would cure his desire for her. If he could just spend some time with her, drink her in, make her come, he could get her out of his system and start fresh on Monday.

Or maybe I'll want her more.

"Oh shit," he uttered as he saw her walk out of her downtown condo toward the black Mercedes from the car service. She was dressed in black leggings with thigh high boots and a fitted, sleeveless shirt that made her

breasts look amazing. Her long hair
was swept into an easy ponytail and
her gold and diamond jewelry
sparkled in the morning light. She
was a goddess.

Fuck. This might be a bad idea.

He held his breath as she came
toward him. He jumped out of the
car and when she saw him, she
smiled, triggering a warm
avalanche of emotions inside him.

What is happening to me?

"Hi," he said.

"Hey," she said. A warm blush
crossed her cheeks. *God, she's
stunning.*

He took her bags and slapped the
top of the car. The trunk popped
open, and he put them inside,
closing it with a soft click.

"You look amazing," he said. *I
want to kiss her. Should I?*

He stepped to her and leaned in.
She welcomed his advance. He first
brushed his lips softly against hers,

then took her lips in his own as he moved deeper into mouth, running his hands up her back.

"Mmmm," she moaned.

His cock stiffened at the noise she made. It didn't take much for her to turn him on and it had been like that since he saw her in the bar only a few nights ago. He was captivated by her.

He pulled back from the kiss and looked into her eyes. "Save some of that for the ride."

"I like that idea," she said.

They crawled into the backseat of the car, and he tapped the blackened divider. A few seconds later, the car started to move.

"So," she said. "Where is this cabin?"

"About twenty minutes north, right on the lake," he said. "Surrounded by beach and nature, and you can see the city."

"I love that," she said.

"I think you will," he said. "Did you bring warm clothes? It can get chilly on the lake."

"I actually did," she said. "I'm used to beachy weather and cool nights."

"Cleveland?"

"That, yes," she said. "And we used to go every year to Top Sail—"

"North Carolina," he interrupted.

"Yeah," she said. "I normally have to tell people that. How'd you know?"

"I love that place," he said. "I like to travel, and I found it when I was driving the coast a couple years ago. Great food. Great little town. Beaches are beautiful. How did you find it?"

"My family used to go there every year."

"Used to?" he asked.

"My parents died in a car crash
when I was 16. Me and my brothers
never went again," she said quietly.

"Oh, Summer, I'm sorry."

"No, no, it's fine. I have
incredible memories there," she
said. She smiled. "I even put in an
offer over the weekend for a little
beach house there. It's small, but I
can afford it. And it would be great
to have a place where I could
remember them in a beautiful
way."

"That's…amazing," he said.
"When will you hear if you got it?"

"Hopefully in the next few
days," she said. He looked over her
face and could see that talking
about the beach house in Top Sail
gave her joy.

"I hope you get it," he said. "I'm
sure your big sale last week helped.
Congrats on that."

"How did you…oh, did Dalia
catch you up?"

"She did," he said. "She said you're one of the best salespersons she's ever seen, this company or anywhere."

"That's kind of her," Summer said.

"Not kind," he said. She looked at him with surprise. "I mean, it's business. She meant it as a compliment to you for your business acumen. And I would agree. Your numbers are unbelievable."

He smiled at her and hoped he was communicating how impressed he was. Because he was. She was a remarkable salesperson, according to the money trail.

"Thank you," she said. She sat up straighter and smiled at him. "I do work hard for it."

"I can see that," he said. "So, you were celebrating Friday night."

He saw a blush cross her cheeks as she grinned at him.

"I was," she said. "Thanks for helping me."

He laughed at that. "My pleasure," he said. "Truly."

She laughed with him. This time when he glanced to her, she moved toward him, sliding her hand under his relaxed T-shirt onto his bare skin. Her touch made him instantly hard, and he leaned in and took her lips in his with a hunger he hadn't felt since his last relationship.

He was closing in on forty and he'd had two serious relationships, the last of which ended two years ago and had been the closest he'd ever gotten to marriage.

Diane had been a year older than him and absolutely perfect. She had been everything to him, and when they'd had a conversation about the next step, they both initially said they wanted marriage. And then, over the course of a few months after feeling the weight of that admission, they both realized they didn't. They loved each other more than anything, and were still friends to this day, but there was something missing. After four years together, neither of them could ignore that anymore.

Their break-up had been painful for him. So painful, he'd fallen into the habit of picking up women and staying a night or two then heading off. But with Summer…he couldn't stop thinking about her. When he'd kissed her that night, it was like something out of one of those chick flicks.

And now, her delicate hand was rubbing his chest with urgency as she skillfully climbed into his lap and straddled him, rubbing his cock between her legs with powerful strides.

"Summer," he moaned.

"Fuck me," she whispered.

He grabbed her cute, round ass and squeezed as he rolled her to the side, grabbing her leggings at the waist and pulling them down around her ankles. She immediately spread her legs and smiled as he dipped into her slit with his tongue and licked hungrily.

Her moan was everything and it made his heart race as he tasted her sweetness. He took his thick fingers and slid them inside her wet pussy as she gasped with pleasure.

"Ace, yes," she moaned.

Hearing his name on her lips made him want to take her. He lifted her legs in the air and slid under her leggings. He settled between her thighs, pulling her hips to him and sliding inside her.

"Summer," he choked out. He could barely contain himself as he thrust inside of her.

"Ace," she moaned as she gripped his back, clawing at him like a hungry animal.

She thrust her body against his as they greedily took each other in the backseat. *This woman. My God.*

He could feel his climax building.

"Summer," he moaned. "I'm coming."

"Yes," she screamed. She gripped his back. "I'm gonna come with you!"

They cried out together with pleasure as their orgasms built and released at the same time. Her thighs gripped his hips as she writhed underneath him.

He finished as she did, then he leaned down and kissed her gently.

"You're amazing," he said.

"You are, too," she whispered.

They chuckled together as they came apart and started to pull their clothes on. Once they were each

fully dressed, she leaned into him
and buried her face into the crook
of his neck. His whole body
warmed to her touch.

As he relaxed into her, the car
came to a stop. They sat there
quietly for a moment.

"We're here," he said.

"I can't wait," she replied."

And neither could he.

5

The Brother

As Summer walked through the lavish lake house, it struck her that this place was more like a mini-mansion than a "house." But it was definitely decorated in her style. The color palette was warm whites, creams, and neutral colors with touches of blue here and there to bring out the water theme. Everything was high-end from the appliances to the fabric.

"It's beautiful," she said.

"Thanks." She felt his stare on her, so she turned to face him.

"Did you do all this?" She waved her hand at the opulence.

"I did, actually," he said. "I rehabbed it. Added a few rooms, knocked down a few walls, worked with the interior designer to get this look and feel."

"Are you also in real estate?"

"I wouldn't say I'm *in* real estate, but I do like to invest in properties. I like the rehabbing part as well."

"You're good at it," she quipped. She smiled broadly at him as he stepped to her and put his arms around her waist giving her a light kiss. She loved the way his lips felt, like velvet. And his kiss was near perfect, soft and gentle, not too wet or dry, never overly intrusive with the tongue.

"Did you eat breakfast?" he asked gently.

"I had a little something," she said. His eyes were blazing with desire as he smiled at her.

"Can I make you something and then we can…"

She smiled. "We can." She glanced out at the lap pool and hot tub area that hosted an enclosed outdoor shower. "I'm pretty sure I'll need another shower after we eat."

She wanted Ace to take her in that outdoor shower and she didn't want to wait long for it. If she only had a week with him, she was going to take advantage of it.

She turned on the heat as she kissed him this time, passionately and deeply with an urgency to have him in her again.

"Summer," he breathed heavily as she pulled away.

"Breakfast first," she teased.

"That's not fair," he said. A laugh escaped his lips. "But have a seat. I'm about to impress you."

"I'm pretty sure you've already done that," she said as she sauntered to the kitchen. "But I'd love to know if you can cook."

"Oh, I can cook," he boasted. He followed her to the kitchen and

started to haul out tools and food
and drinks. He made her a mimosa
and dropped a couple raspberries in
it for effect.

"Nice," she said. She took a sip.
"And lovely. Alright, let's see these
skills."

"Your wish," he said. He
cracked a few eggs into a bowl and
started whipping them with a little
milk. "My command."

"You have no idea," she smiled
with wicked heat.

A heat passed between them as
he cooked her breakfast and she
thought about everything she
wanted him to do to her after.

~~~

As she dropped her fork onto her
plate, she said, "Ace…this
was…wow. Where'd you learn to
cook?"
~~~

"My mom," he said. "She told me and my brother we needed to know how to cook and take care of ourselves. I can do laundry, too."

"Oh yeah?" she said raising a haughty eyebrow. "I have a hard time believing a man like you does his own laundry."

His deep laugh tingled her ears with delight. *He has such a beautiful laugh. Joyful.*

"You got me," he said. "I do have help and she does manage my dry cleaning, which most of my clothes are, and the laundry. But, when Millie goes on vacation, I do it myself. I have a certain way I like it."

"Softener sheets?"

"You know it," he said. "That little bear really sells it. Makes everything smell good. And soft."

She was the one to laugh to now as she took in the crinkles around his eyes when he smiled and the way his tall, lean body would relax when she grinned back at him. *I like him. A lot. Shoot. One week, Summer, that's it.*

"So," she said. She stood and stretched her curvy body. "I'd love a tour of the outdoor shower."

He stood up and walked toward her, closing the distance with a hunger in his eyes. When he got to her, he lightly touched her body, slowly sliding his hands under her shirt, then her bra, and achingly rubbing her nipples as his hot gaze burned down at her.

"I'd love to give you a tour."

He leaned in and lightly touched her lips with his, using his tongue to part them and kiss her deeply. She couldn't help the light moan that escaped her throat.

"You're going to do a lot more of that," he said. He pulled away and took her hand as he led her across the living room and into the outdoor space.

It was beautiful outside. The area was completely enclosed by towering wood planks wrapped in greenery and flowers. It was like a domesticated jungle with sizzling water elements that spoke of nothing but a good time.

The hot tub was perfect for two and the lap pool was a gorgeous shade of turquoise. The outdoor shower was large with no door and only one wall that held the shower head. There was a bench with two heights, one for sitting and one for…

"I want to fuck you right there," he said with heat as he turned and grabbed her, plopping her on the elevated side of the bench and spreading her legs. "Let's get these clothes off."

He pulled her boots off and tossed them to the side along with her boot socks. He slowly peeled her leggings off as she took her top off. He rubbed his hands up her body as he slid them under her bra grabbing her breasts with a wonderful pressure as his thumbs rubbed her nipples.

"Yes," she panted. His hands were strong as they rubbed her body with delicious abandon. "More."

He stripped off her bra as she returned the favor, tugging off his T-shirt and unbuttoning his jeans. She gasped with delight as he took off his pants. Commando again.

"You oppose underwear?" she flirted.

"Always," he said. "They get in the way."

"Yes, they do," she said breathily as she admired his huge member. It was a wonderfully thick piece of meat with a slight curve that hit all the right places when he

was inside her. She wanted to taste
him.

As he threw his own clothing
aside, she climbed off the bench
and got down on her knees. The
soft mat under them was
comfortable as she took the tip of
him in her mouth with a moan. He
tasted good, salty and sexy.

"Fuck, Summer," he panted.
"Yes, more."

She took him deeper and deeper
in her mouth as his hips moved
slowly in time with her swallows.
God, he tastes so good.

"Summer," he moaned. "That
feels fucking fantastic."

She swallowed him deeper and
felt his moan vibrate in her mouth.

"Stop," he said. "Stop, or I'll
come."

She let him slide out of her
mouth. "Fuck me," she ordered.

"Your wish," he said.

He helped her up and then bent her over the bench as he slid deep inside her.

His thrusts felt amazing as the sunshine poured down on them and the wind swept over their bodies. There was something very animalistic about sex outside and she loved it.

"More," she moaned as he pounded against her body. "Your balls feel so good."

"You like that?" he asked as he gave her one hard thrust and held himself there inside her.

"Yes!"

He did it again. "Like that?"

"God, yes!" she yelled. "More!"

And he pounded her like that before stopping and turning her around.

"Don't stop," she panted.

"I'm not," he said smoothly. He backed her further into the shower, turning on the warm water. She gasped as it rushed over them, its strong streams erotically kneading her body. She gasped again as his hands slid over her wet body, one hand landing on her throat and gently running his fingers up and down it as he kissed her.

She was as wet as the shower now and wanted nothing more than him inside her. As if reading her mind, he reached his hands down around her hips and lifted her against the shower wall.

"Ace, yes," she moaned. "Yes, baby."

"Oh, baby," he said. He slid his cock inside her as she spread her legs wider. "God you're wet."

He drove deep inside her and stayed there, giving her small pulses of that beautiful cock, hitting her G-spot again and again as she writhed with pleasure. She could feel her orgasm building as she grabbed onto his back with one hand and slid her other hand between her legs, rubbing her clit as he thrust.

"I'm gonna come," she said. Her fingers quickened on her clit as he pulsed harder and harder. "That's it."

"God, yes," he moaned. "I'm gonna come."

She came first. The powerful orgasm spread through her body like wildfire as he pulled out and came all over her thighs and stomach.

"Summer," he moaned. "Fuck."

She moved her hand from her clit to his cock and helped finish him off, loving the come that dripped all over her hand.

"Ace, yes," she said silkily.

He slowly put her down and they laughed as they rinsed each other off and kissed gently.

"Should we go out on the lake?" he asked.

"Absolutely."

He turned off the shower and led her back into the living room, leaving their clothes outside.

"Did you bring a suit?" he asked.

"Yep," she said. "Where did you put my bags?"

"The bedroom," he said. He turned and smiled at her. "Follow me."

"Ready so soon?" she asked teasingly.

"Nice try," he said with a laugh. "But no."

As he turned to walk down the hallway to the bedroom, she caught her breath. There on the coffee table was a photo of his family. It was Ace, a woman who looked like his mother, a man who appeared to be his father, and what looked like his brother.

"Oh shit," she said under her breath. She knew his brother. Ace's little brother was Damian. Damian had been her college boyfriend of two months. And her first. *This can't be happening.*

"Great," she mumbled as she followed Ace down the hallway. "Just great."

I can't believe I slept with his brother.

She pondered whether she should tell him or not. If this was only a fling for a week and then back to business on Monday, it wouldn't really matter, would it? Who cares if she slept with his brother at age eighteen, as part of a short-term relationship that didn't mean a whole lot?

But it's not feeling like that.

From his warm eyes and making her breakfast, to calling him baby and a feeling that was growing in her gut, she suddenly felt like it was more than sex. And she wanted to tell him about his brother, to start with total honesty.

Start what?

No, she would just wait and see how it went. If the moment felt right, she'd tell him.

Otherwise, this is a one-week thing, so I'll just keep it to myself.

6

To Tell or Not to Tell

Ace hadn't taken a woman out on his little speed boat since his break-up with Diane two years ago. Summer was the first, and now he was hoping to take her many more times.

Except I made it clear we'd only have this one week.

It was hard to keep that promise as he gazed at her now, sitting at the front of his boat, lazily lying back in the seat, her Pilates legs crossed at the ankles.

She was wearing a simple black swimsuit, high cut at the hips, low-cut in the front and back, both concealing and revealing her body in ways that made him stiffen up every time he glanced at her.

Her chocolate brown hair was swept into a loose bun on top of her head and her aviator sunglasses made her look like a celebrity.

She's gorgeous.

He pulled into a private cove and stopped the boat, then dropped an anchor to keep them there. It was one of his favorite spots to dock for lunch, complete with a little beach and trees for shade.

"How's this spot for lunch?" he asked. "You like it?"

"Perfect," she said. She rose from her seat and walked up to him, sliding her arms around his waist, and leaning into him for a kiss. He obliged, gently kissing her and rubbing her back.

"You hungry?" he asked softly.

"Starving."

"Have a seat, then."

He grabbed a packed picnic basket and started pulling out the food.

"Look at you." She laughed. "You're spoiling me."

"I am," he said. "I like to."

He brought out seltzer water, wine, a tomato-mozzarella salad, grilled chicken salads, and rosemary bread. He set up a plate for her and she took it with a smile.

"Thank you," she said. She dug in as he took a sip of wine and sat down next to her. "This is delicious."

"Thank you," he said. He started eating his own food. "So, you said have brothers. How many?"

"Four," she said. She took a sip of wine and laughed.

"Wow, four," he said. "I thought one little brother was enough."

He noticed a strange look on her face when he mentioned his little brother. "What?"

"Oh, nothing," she said. "Yeah, our house was noisy. And I'm the youngest, so they're very protective of me."

"As they should be," he said. He took another sip of wine.

"So," she said, putting down her wine. "Have you ever been married?"

"Close," he said. "Diane. I loved her. Very much. But…it wasn't quite…it. You know?"

"I do," she said.

"You ever been married?"

"Oh, no," she said quickly.

He laughed as he swallowed his food. "Tell me how you really feel."

"Right?" She laughed. "I just wanted to be focused on my career and make some money. After our parents died, my oldest brother, Dustin, and his wife, had me move in with them until I graduated high school."

"That must have been tough."
He eyed her face as her expression
took on a thoughtful look.

"It was hard to lose them," she
said. She shifted in her seat and
smiled at him. "But, I was lucky. I
had my brothers."

"Are you still close?"

"Very," she said. "Dustin has a
daughter. She's five. And adorable.
And acts thirty."

"Of course she does," he said.
He smiled at the look on her face
when she talked about her niece.

"I take her on shopping trips and
to the park and we adopted a kitten
last week."

She shrugged at him with a grin.

"I bet your brother loved that."

"He was pissed," she said. "And
then he saw the little, white
fluffball and fell in love. Her name
is Snowball."

"Sounds about right."

"I try to do things with her that I think my mom would have done, you know?" She grinned at him sheepishly. "I still remember when my mom took me to get a kitten for the first time. You remember those things."

He reached over and caressed her face and when he did, she leaned into his hand and rubbed her head against it. In that moment, he wanted nothing more than to protect her. He leaned over and kissed her gently.

"I'm sorry, Summer."

"It's okay," she said quietly. They both leaned back and smiled.

"So, what about you?" she asked. "Are you close to your family?"

"Incredibly close," he said. He took a sip of wine. "My parents have been married forty years. They act like teenagers still."

"That's so sweet." She leaned toward him, and he had a hard time focusing when she gazed at him like that.

"Yeah, they're great," he said. "And my little brother and I are really close. He's maybe two or three years older than you. Are you around twenty-eight? Twenty-nine?"

"I'm twenty-eight," she said.

"Yeah, he's thirty," he said.

"And you are?"

"I'm thirty-seven," he said. "So, growing up, I was protective of my little brother, you know? Take him places. Show him stuff. Take care of any bullies."

"Tough guy, eh?"

"Sometimes," he laughed. "I guess when I needed to be."

He noticed a look crossed her face, like the one from earlier when he mentioned his brother. He crinkled his forehead. "What?"

"I think," she said. She shifted uncomfortably. "I think I need to tell you something."

"Oh," he said. He sat back and gave her his full attention. "Okay. What is it?"

"Your brother," she said. "I know him."

"You do? How?"

"We went to the same college."

"Oh," he said. "Ohio State. Were you friends or something?"

He knew immediately from the look on her face it was definitely more than friendship. His heart dropped.

Please, just don't say it was serious, was all he could think as she told him the story.

7

Talk to Me

Summer knew the minute they took off on the boat that she was going to tell Ace about Damian. That feeling only intensified as they ate lunch together and talked.

Ace was open and warm with a genuine concern for her and her feelings. She felt so safe with him and protected. And the sex…it was the best she'd ever had.

She knew dating her boss would be a terrible idea. But the thought of not seeing him like this, of not having sex with him, of not talking to him, was suddenly no longer an option.

So, when he started talking about his family and his brother, she knew this was her moment.

"I was a freshman at Ohio State when he was a junior," she explained. "It was short-lived. We only dated a few months, had a lot of fun, but that's it. We stayed friendly after when we'd see each other, but…it wasn't serious."

He seemed relieved to hear that as a breath escaped his lips.

"Oh, okay, good," he said. "So, just a college thing, then?"

"Yeah," she said. She squirmed a little. "There is one more thing. In full disclosure."

"Okay, shoot," he said.

"Uh, well," she said. "He was my first."

"In college?" he asked. "Or ever?"

"Ever," she said.

"Ah, okay," he said. "That's…okay."

She watched as he took a long sip of his wine. There was an awkward silence until he finally said, "I mean, that was years ago, Summer. And it wasn't serious. So…"

"So, you're okay?"

"I'm totally fine," he said. "And I appreciate you telling me."

"Oh," she said. She felt the tone of disappointment in her voice, and she wasn't sure why it was there. She should feel good about the fact that he wasn't going to be mad about the Damian thing and that it wasn't going to interfere with a relationship between them.

But, dammit, he could at least react a little, right? Because if he didn't react, that meant he didn't feel jealousy. And if he wasn't jealous, then it was because he didn't care. Right?

Which means I care more than he does.

She grabbed a wine and took an annoyed sip.

"Summer?" he asked. "You okay?"

"Yeah," she said tersely. "Good."

She put her wine down and looked anywhere but at him.

"You don't' seem good," he said softly.

"I mean," she said. She could hear how tense her voice was and she wasn't quite sure what she was getting all worked up about. But she couldn't help the anxiety building in her gut. "You don't care at all?"

She directed an angry stare right at him.

"Do you want me to care about it?" he asked.

"You could at least…" she trailed off. She tugged a loose hair behind her ear. "It doesn't matter."

"It clearly does matter," he said. "Talk to me, Summer. What's going on? What's *really* going on here?"

A sigh escaped her lips as she turned to face him. When she took in those warm eyes and caring stare her breath caught. She was not getting out of this unscathed, she knew that now. She had avoided moments like this all her life, staying laser-focused on her career, and now, she couldn't avoid it any longer. Not with this man.

For the first time in her life, she was starting to truly fall for someone. For Ace. Her soon-to-be-boss. Her mother fucking boss. Her career and her love life were in direct contradiction, the thing she had tried to avoid. And she wasn't sure how to handle that.

"I just…I wasn't expecting you," she said.

She appreciated the wide smile that her admission elicited from him. Maybe there *was* hope.

"I wasn't expecting you, either," he said. "Is that a bad thing?"

"No, it's a great thing," she said. "A really great thing. But…this thing with us is on a timer and, I guess, I don't want it to be. And I thought, maybe, you wouldn't want it to be, either. But then you didn't react to me telling you about your brother, like…like maybe this doesn't mean as much to you as it does to me. I guess that's why I'm reacting like this."

"Oh," he said softly.

They stared at each other for a moment as the acknowledgement of their attraction to each other in a real, meaningful way sunk in. When she saw his gaze shift from consideration to glancing away, her gut sank.

"Just tell me now if you don't' feel the same way," she demanded.

"It's not that, Summer," he said.

"Then what is it?" she asked.

"You know what it is."

"Because you're my boss."

"Yeah," he said. "Listen, I have never crossed that line. Ever. I would never. Integrity means a great deal to me, and I wouldn't risk it in my career. And, clearly, you wouldn't, either. You're laser-focused on your career. I can't imagine anything being more important than that right now, based on your numbers."

"Yeah, you're right, I haven't," she said. "But, this is different."

"It is, I know," he said. "And I know we didn't realize the situation when we met. But we know it now. And I don't want to start on the wrong foot. For me or you. And Summer…"

He waited until she looked at him.

"You know as well as I do, this will be worse for you," he said. "I mean, it would be bad for both of us, of course. But the world is especially hard on women with these things, for no good reason, in my opinion. It takes two, you know?"

Her whole heart sunk in her chest as she acknowledged his statements. He was right, of course. She knew he was right.

"I wanna go home," she said.

"Oh," he said quietly.

"I mean, I don't," she said. She looked at the pained expression on his face. "But that's why I do."

"I'll call the car service when we get back."

"Okay," she said quietly. She glanced at him and the food he'd prepared and the lake surrounding them. She felt her body respond to the way his strong hands clasped each other as his eyes stared down at his feet.

"Ace?"

"Yeah?" he asked. He looked up at her and the conflicting emotions in his eyes tugged at her heart.

"Maybe…call them in the morning?"

She knew that was probably a bad idea, too, to stay one more night. It was like prolonging the inevitable. But she needed one more night with him. And he obviously needed it with her, given the wide smile that took over his face.

"I'd like that," he said. "If you're sure."

"I'm sure," she said. "I want one more night with you. So…you better make it count."

She laughed a little to cut the tension and he did, too.

"I'll make it count for both of us," he said.

"Good," she said.

"Head back?" he asked.

She nodded as they both moved to clean up. He lightly touched her hands.

"I got it," he said. "Just sit back and relax."

She smiled, leaning back into her seat, and watching him clean up. She would pretend. She would pretend that everything was perfectly okay. That starting tomorrow Ace was just her boss. And that she would be just his employee and that they were both fine with that.

After all, that's how she got through her parent's death— pretending she was fine. So, that's what she would do now.

Tonight, Ace was her lover. Tomorrow, he was her boss.

And everything was just fine.

8

Change of Heart

The ride back to Summer's house was agonizing. Ace knew he didn't want this to be over, the same as her. But what was he supposed to do? As of Monday, she was his employee, and he didn't want to kick off his new venture with rumors and innuendos.

He glanced at her from his side of the Mercedes. Her hair was down today and wavy. It gently cascaded over her shoulders, touching her ample breasts, which were caged in a simple pink tank top. Her curvy hips were shifted away from him, which gave him a perfect view of her ass. Today, it was wrapped in light blue jeans.

He couldn't shake the memory
of grabbing those hips last night
and thrusting deep inside her from
behind as she moaned. They started
in the kitchen, against the table
after dinner, and moved to the pool
under the moonlight. He'd spread
her legs wide and sunk inside her
as the water splashed around them
and her breasts rubbed his chest.

He had taken her nipples in his
mouth and sucked on them, then
caressed them with his tongue as
she came. He came inside her again
and again. The view of his cum
dripping down her thighs as she
stepped out of the pool and walked
toward the house had him hard as
he followed.

They ended up in the bedroom
where he'd taken her again, firmly
lying between her legs and gazing
into her eyes as she whispered his
name. She'd done that again this
morning and he couldn't shake the

way his name sounded on her lips. Her low, raspy voice whispering it as he moved inside her nearly overtook him.

"Summer," he finally said. She turned her head toward him, acknowledging he'd said her name, but refusing to look at him. And he didn't know what to say anyway. "Nevermind, I guess."

What was he going to do? Marry her? He just met her. He wanted to date her. Explore her. Fall for her. And he knew if he spent any more time with her, that's exactly where it was headed.

I'm gonna fall in love with her.

He glanced at her again as they pulled up to her condo.

"I guess this is goodbye," she said.

"Mmmhmm," he mumbled. "I guess it is."

After an awkward moment he said, "I'll help you with your bags."

As he went to open his door, she lightly touched his arm.

"No, Ace," she said quietly. "Let's just say goodbye now, okay?"

He nodded. "Summer—"

"Goodbye, Ace," she said.

She climbed out of the car and grabbed her bags from the trunk. His heart sunk as she walked away from him. *Why the hell did I take this job anyway?*

~~~

Summer paced across her living room floor as thoughts of the last six days ran on an agonizing loop in her brain.

Logically, she got it. Emotionally, her heart was breaking. Ace was the first man in her life that she could suddenly picture something real with.
~~~

Something perfect, something that looked a lot like what real love might look like. It reminded her of her parents and the love they'd had together. It hadn't been perfect, of course, but it had been perfect for them.

She grabbed a tissue as her eyes misted over. These were the moments she missed her mother the most. This was a conversation she would have called her mom and begged for advice.

"Mom," she would have said. "What do I do?"

She imagined her mother's warm voice comforting her and saying something like, "Could he be the one for you?"

And Summer would have had answered, "Yes."

And she guessed her mother would have said, "You can always get another job. You can't always find another love."

Or maybe that was just Summer's eager heart wishing for something she wasn't going to have with Ace.

She picked up her phone to dial Annie.

Annie had been her best friend all throughout college. They'd met their freshman year and roomed together sophomore and junior years. Their senior year, Annie had lived with her boyfriend for the fall semester, and when they broke up, she'd lived with Summer in the spring. Annie had been from Columbus and after they graduated, she moved to Cleveland. They'd roomed for two more years together before Annie met Tommy. And then, well…Tommy.

Annie was like the sister she never had, and a loyal friend. As she dialed her friend's number, her Ring app went off, followed by a knock at her door.

"What the hell?" she whispered.

She glanced at the app and her whole gut twisted into a kaleidoscope of emotions. She jogged to the door, swung it open, and without asking why he came back, she wrapped her arms around Ace's neck and kissed him deeply.

"Summer," he choked out. They tumbled through the door and into her condo, kissing passionately.

"Summer," he said again, stopping her, and gently pushing her away as they both caught their breaths.

"Ace," she said. She could barely breathe.

"Just, let's talk for a second," he said.

They both peered at each other and then started laughing.

"This is a bad fucking idea," he said. His laughing stopped and he smiled at her.

"A terrible fucking idea," she said.

She grinned back at him.

"Look, I don't know what to do," he said. "But I do know, I want to spend the rest of the week with you. And Sunday night, we can have a real talk about what to do Monday morning. Okay?"

"Okay," she said quietly.

They gazed at each other with humor and genuine affection.

"But Ace," she said.

"Yeah?"

"You should know, this thing between us—it really does mean something to me," she said. "I'm starting to care…to fall—"

"I know," he interrupted. "Me, too."

Her heart leapt into her throat as he smiled and walked toward her. His eyes were filled with joy as he took her in his arms.

"We have five days together before we figure out what to do next," he said. "So, what do you say we make 'em count?"

"I like that idea," she said. She beamed with happiness and wrapped her arms around his neck. "How about we start with me making you lunch? I'm a pretty good cook, too."

"I have no doubt," he said with a chuckle.

"Alright, then, let's eat."

She led him to the kitchen and could feel that whatever this was, it had officially started.

And there was no turning back.

9

Breakfast of Champions

Summer woke up Saturday morning and couldn't remember the last time she'd been this happy. There had never been a man who had made her feel so taken care of on every level possible. Her mind, her heart, and most definitely everything between her legs.

They'd christened almost every room in her condo and then in his house, spending time cooking, shopping, visiting places in Cleveland she hadn't ever been, even though she grew up here.

Ace had also called his brother and broached the subject of Damian and Summer's college relationship. They'd had a good talk and she'd said hello to Damian herself. He gave them his blessing, which was easy since he was married now with a baby on the way.

"God, that was so long ago," Damian had laughed. "You don't need my permission. We're all adults here. And what Summer and I had was so brief…I wish you both the best."

She and Ace had laughed and thanked him, and then the brothers had started talking about family stuff and Summer went and made dinner. After the marinated chicken and twice baked potatoes, they cracked open a nice port and had a few sips in front of the fireplace. He'd taken her glass and set it on the table, then turned and slid his hand between her legs.

"Ace," she had moaned. He had slowly slid her clothes off, then his, and got on his knees, burying his face deep in her sensitive folds, licking her slit with powerful thrusts of his tongue and making her come. As soon as she did, he'd flipped her over on her knees and she grabbed the back of the couch. Her nipples had rubbed against the fabric erotically as he fucked her deeply and wildly.

"Spread your legs wider," he'd ordered.

"Yes, baby," she'd said submissively. "Tell me what else to do."

"Lift your ass higher," he said. He gave her a light slap on the ass as she moaned.

"Yes, baby," she said enthusiastically. She lifted her ass higher and when she did, she felt his cock slide even deeper, hitting her G-spot as her wetness made a delicious smacking sound. "God yes, baby! Smack my ass again!"

And he had. He gave her a nice, hard smack right on the ass and

when he did, it made her orgasm
rise to the brink.

"Again!" she ordered. And he
smacked her ass again, harder this
time. When he did, it gave her a jolt
that made her come hard. "I'm
coming!"

"I'm coming, too," he yelled.
And she felt him grab her hips and
drive his cock deep as his come
poured inside of her.

"Come in me, baby," she said as
her climax peaked and slowed.
"Fill me up."

"Fuck, yes," he said. She felt his
grip loosen. "God, Summer."

After that, he'd carried her to the
bedroom and they fell asleep in
each other's arms, waking up that
way, too.

And now, it was Saturday.
Tomorrow was "the talk." And she
could feel the anxiety building in
her gut.

*I don't wanna let him go. But
how can we possibly fix this?*

"Hey beautiful," he said. He
walked in with McDonald's
pancakes and fresh coffee.
"Hungry?"

"Famished," she said. She sat up
brightly. "How could I not be after
last night?"

"And the night before?" he
asked sexily.

"And the night before?" she
responded.

He made it to the bed, put the
food on the side table, and slid in.
He gently took her face in his
hands and gave her a light kiss.

"This has been the best week of
my life," he said. "I mean that."

"Me, too," she said.

There was a long silence as they
gazed at each other, each knowing
what tomorrow meant.

"Summer—"

"Not yet, Ace," she said. "Not until tomorrow."

He nodded. "Okay."

He turned away and grabbed the coffee, handing it to her.

"Black, one sweetener," he said.

"Thank you."

Then he grabbed the pancakes and dropped them on the bed, a plastic container for each of them.

"Nothing's better than McDonald's hotcakes," he said. He grinned at her.

"Breakfast of champions," she said.

"Let's eat," he said. As they started to open their containers he glanced at her. "I'd like to take you out to dinner tonight. Someplace nice. Romantic."

She stuffed a huge bite of pancake in her mouth right as he asked. She smiled broadly, her cheeks stuffed with pancakes.

"Okay," she said with her mouth full.

He laughed. "You're adorable."

"Thank you," she said as she swallowed. "So, I get to be all dressed up then?"

"Absolutely," he said. It was his turn to talk with a mouth full of pancakes.

She paused for a second. "Do you think it's a good idea to go out to dinner in public right now?"

"We've been out and about all this week," he said.

"True," she said. "But mostly during work hours when no one is out. This is date night."

"It *is* date night," he said. He turned a smoldering stare her direction. "And we're going on a date."

She nodded at him with a smile. "Okay," she said quietly. She glanced at him and then the food. "So, where's the sausage?"

"Right here." He grabbed another bag from the side table.

"There it is," she said.

"A woman after my own heart." He smiled as he gave her the sausage and a sweet stare.

She wanted nothing more than to go on this date with him. But it was gnawing at her gut that they would be caught before they were ready to explain. And what then?

She smiled back at him, remembering every wonderful moment they'd spent together.

For now, she didn't care what anyone else thought. And if she was honest, she wasn't sure she ever would.

~~~

Ace was fairly certain he was going to have a hard time sitting through dinner with Summer.
~~~

When she'd walked out in her first dress, a stunning emerald number that showed off her legs and that deliciously curvy ass, he'd taken her right then and there, accidentally ripping her dress and mussing her hair.

When she came out in her second dress, a silky navy-blue number with a slit up the leg and an open back that dipped all the way to her waist, he was certain he was going to ruin that dress, too.

"Don't even think about it," she had said. They had laughed and quickly walked out the door before their animal instincts could take over.

Sitting in this atmospheric restaurant with candlelight and soft music, he wanted her again. But even more than that, he wanted to sweep her in his arms and just never let go. He was falling hard for her, and their conversation tomorrow night would be a difficult one.

What was he going to do? He'd never met anyone like Summer, and he wasn't about to lose her, so staying in this relationship with her was his choice. Which meant, he had to decide what to do about work.

"What are you thinking about?" she asked.

Her peered up at her and took in the way the candles lit her face with a beautiful amber light, the dancing flames reflecting in her liquid brown eyes.

"You know what I'm thinking about," he said softly.

The smile on her face disappeared for a moment before she nodded. "I know. Me, too."

"Summer, I—"

"Summer?"

Ace didn't see who had called Summer's name, but he saw

Summer's face. It looked like she'd just gotten caught robbing a bank, so he had a guess it was Dalia before Summer's boss even appeared at their table.

"Dalia," Summer said quietly.

Dalia glanced at Summer and then Ace.

"Ace," Dalia said with a nod.

"Dalia," Ace returned. "Look, we can—"

"Summer, can I speak with you?"

Dalia walked away toward the bar area as Summer glanced at Ace.

"Summer—"

"It's okay, Ace," she interrupted. "Really. I'll be fine. I'll be right back, okay?"

He nodded. He watched as Summer stood and walked to meet Dalia at the bar. He couldn't tell what was being said but he knew it wasn't good. Dalia's serious face as she spoke with Summer was enough to tell him that Dalia thought this was a bad idea. But the worst part was Summer's face as she walked back. Whatever Dalia had said to Summer, Summer had taken it to heart.

"What'd she say?" he asked as Summer sat down.

"Let's talk about it tomorrow," she said softly. She swallowed hard, then shook it off, giving him her best smile. "I want to have an amazing night with you, okay?"

He saw in her eyes an incredible warmth and desire to do just that. So, he let it go.

"Okay," he agreed. "To tonight."

He raised his drink and she raised hers. As they clinked them together, he felt a tugging anxiety at his gut.

I'm gonna lose her. And I can't lose her.

10

Do You Want Love?

Summer had tossed and turned all night, as did Ace. They'd wake up and each would pretend they were asleep. Then they'd go back to their private thoughts and squirm some more.

This morning, they'd gotten up and went about getting dressed quietly, the silence a heavy reminder that the week they'd given each other was coming to a close and what was left was a difficult conversation about what to do next.

That answer had been easy for Summer on Saturday morning. On Saturday morning, eating pancakes in bed with him, she didn't care what anyone thought. Ace was the person she wanted to be her partner, to see where it could go, to keep dating and have a serious relationship with.

And then Saturday night had come, and Dalia had crushed that reality in a few short seconds.

"Do you want love?" Dalia had asked her after discovering the two of them at dinner. "Or do you want to further your career? Because this ends badly for both of you."

"But, Dalia, we met before we even knew each other," Summer argued. "That's not the same as starting a relationship at work or because of the power indifference. It's not the same."

"It doesn't matter," Dalia had said.

"I think it does," Summer had said. "I don't want to lose him."

"I'm not going to give you the promotion if you continue this relationship," Dalia had said. "It will look bad for me and for the company and for you."

"I earned that promotion, Dalia," Summer had said angrily. "I worked my ass off for it."

"I'm not saying you didn't," she countered. "I'm saying that it will look bad if this gets out and—"

"And nothing," Summer had said. "Everyone at that company knows I earned that promotion. And I met Ace before I knew who he was. And I'm not letting him go."

"It's your choice," Dalia had said. "But I'm not changing my mind about this. So, make your decision and let me know Monday."

And then she had walked away in a huff. Summer had been confused by the whole thing. She thought Dalia would have been an ally for her, someone she could confide in about next steps, so her dismissive attitude had been a shock. And now she didn't know what to do.

"Summer?"

She stopped making breakfast long enough to look up into Ace's eyes.

"I think we should go ahead and talk," he said quietly.

She nodded, putting down her kitchen utensils, and taking his hand as he led her to the kitchen table in her condo.

They sat across from each other, each looking worse for the wear.

"Summer, I don't wanna lose you," he said. His expression was warm and genuine. "My choice is that we stay together. I mean that. I want a relationship with you."

"And what do you propose to do about work?"

"I haven't figured it out yet," he said. "But I'd like to talk with the head of H.R. tomorrow and discuss

the possibilities. If it comes down
to it, I'll leave the company."

"No, you can't do that," she said.
"You're important to the growth of
this company. So many people's
jobs and livelihoods and families
are depending on this expansion
and new direction you're taking
us."

"You're important to this
company, too, and those same
people," he said. "The sales you
make are what keeps our teams
employed, Summer. I can't grow
this company without you and
salespeople like you."

They stared at each other for a
moment.

"Summer, what do you want?"
he asked directly. "Tell me. The
truth."

"Yesterday morning I would
have told you I wanted the exact
same thing," she said.

"And now?" he pressed. "What did Dalia say to you?"

She took a deep breath and smiled at him.

"Now, if I told you that, then it would highlight the exact reason why we shouldn't be dating in the first place," Summer said. "I'm not going to pit my boss and you against each other. She had every right to say what she said."

He smiled at her and this time it looked different.

"What?" she asked.

"I," he started. He let out a sigh. "I'm impressed you said that. I respect it. A lot."

Respect. She knew he thought she was a badass, that he respected her sales numbers, he'd said it one hundred times over. But now, he respected her, as a person, as a team member, as part of the business. And that felt even better to be respected as a colleague, too.

She grinned back at him.

"I'm falling for you, Ace," she said.

She felt joy spread across her chest as his eyes lit with happiness.

"I'm falling for you, too," he said quietly.

She nodded. "But I don't know what to do here. I love my career. I've worked hard for everything I've got. I can't just throw it away. And I know you understand that."

His smile faded as he realized that she was still torn.

"I do," he agreed.

They sat quietly for a moment.

"Whatever we decide, Summer, we should do it tomorrow. Because after that, it really does become an H.R. issue," he said. "Right now, we haven't done anything wrong. My start day is when it crosses a line unless I notify H.R. right away that we had a pre-existing relationship."

She nodded in agreement with him. He was absolutely correct and she knew that.

"If this had just been about sex, then ending it would make all the sense in the world," he said. "But this isn't that. This is real, Summer. At least it is for me."

She smiled at him.

"It is for me, too," she said.

"Well, then," he said. "What do we do?"

11

Monday Morning

Summer's stomach was in knots as she marched her way to Dalia's office. She didn't how this was all going to play out, but she was prepared for the consequences either way.

She and Ace had gone back and forth all of Sunday afternoon about how to approach the situation and what to do. They talked about ending it, about telling everyone, about telling no one, and none of the options seemed right. Finally, Ace had brought an end to it when he said, "I'm talking to H.R. in the morning and that's the end of it. This is my responsibility as the CEO. And I don't want you taking any heat for it."

She had been a little stunned at his abruptness, but she nodded at him and agreed to it. Mostly because H.R. would tell him what his next steps should be in a way that was fair to him, to Summer, and to the company. And once he knew their point of view, the two of them would have more information and could make a better decision.

After they had decided, she'd pulled off his clothes and climbed on his hard cock as her wetness made him slide in and out of her at a slick, frantic pace.

"Summer," he'd moaned as she'd leaned down onto him and rubbed her aching nipples against his chest. She had kissed him deeply then as he grabbed her ass and squeezed, giving it a playful slap and spreading her wider so he could fill her deeper.

"Yes, baby," she'd moaned as her hips thrust against harder.

"I'm coming," he'd said. His cock was so hard she could feel it rubbing roughly against all of her insides. It made her pussy tingle in all the right ways as she came with him.

"Baby, I'm coming," she'd yelled. And as she did, he pulled her nipple into his mouth and sucked hard as he slapped her ass, making her come again. "Fuck!"

They'd fallen asleep after that and woke up in each other's arms, ready to face whatever was coming.

And now was that time.

As Summer turned from the hallway into Dalia's office, she took a deep breath.

"Dalia," Summer said sternly as her boss turned from the computer to face her.

"Summer, stop," Dalia said, standing up. "Before you say anything."

Dalia crossed the office and shut the door behind Summer, coming around to stand in front of her.

"I'm sorry about Saturday night," she said.

"Wait, what?" Summer asked with surprise. She let her guard down as she took in Dalia's apologetic stare. "But I thought—"

"I had an affair with my boss when I was twenty-five," Dalia said.

"Oh," Summer said. "I see."

Dalia leaned against her desk as she gave a weak smile to Summer.

"My career at that company did not survive that affair," Dalia said. "He, on the other hand, is the CEO now."

Summer gave a nod. "Gotcha."

An understanding passed between them.

"It's not the same for women," Dalia said. "It's better now, of course. But…it's still not the same.

And, honestly, it's not good for
either person."

Summer nodded.

"And that's where it was coming
from on Saturday night," she said.
She crossed her arms. "And I was
surprised, you know?"

"I understand," Summer said.
"But, Dalia, it's not the same
thing."

Dalia nodded. "Yeah, on Sunday
morning, I started to think maybe it
wasn't," she said. "I've known you
a long time, Summer. And I know
you don't give your heart away
easily, or at all."

She smiled at Summer as
Summer felt her body start to relax.

"So, if you made a choice to be
out in public with Ace, to be with
Ace, period," Dalia raised her
hands in a questioning motion. "It
must be something special. At least
to you. I don't know him well
enough to make that call, but—"

"He's talking to H.R. now," Summer said.

"He is?" Dalia asked.

"He seems to think that because we started our relationship before he started, and that we didn't know each other when it started, which we didn't, that we may be able to find a way to make it work," Summer said hopefully.

Dalia sighed. "I hope so, Summer. You seemed…happy on Saturday."

"I am," Summer said quietly.

"A relationship, huh?" Dalia asked.

Summer looked up and saw Dalia smiling at her. Summer nodded. "Yeah."

"That makes me happy for you," Dalia said quietly. "Plus, it'll be nice to have someone you can celebrate your promotion with."

Dalia got up, turned, and sat back down at her desk.

"Promotion?" Summer asked. Her face lit up with excitement.

"Didn't I tell you? I submitted you this morning," Dalia said earnestly. "You earned it. You really did. Congratulations."

Summer smiled broadly at her boss. "Thank you, Dalia."

"Get outta here," she said. "Go make us some more money, huh?"

"I'm on it," Summer said.

She felt like she was floating on a cloud as she made her way back to her office. She didn't think it could get any better as she turned into her office. Wrong again.

"Hey gorgeous," Ace said smoothly as he stood from his sitting position on the edge of her desk.

"Hey sexy," she said. Then she put her hand over her mouth quickly before adding, "I probably shouldn't say that here."

"No," he said. "You shouldn't."

He smiled at her as he closed the distance between them.

"I spoke with the head of H.R.," he said. "I disclosed our relationship and explained how we met."

"Oh my God," she said. She could feel the blush slide up her neck.

"I didn't disclose that, Summer," he said. He laughed. "I just meant I disclosed that when we met, we didn't realize who the other was, and our dating started before today."

"And what they'd say?" she asked. She held her breath.

"I had to recuse myself from any discussions about your career," he said. "I can't be part of discussions about your promotions, your work, your assignments, your clients, nothing. The COO will handle all that from a leadership perspective."

"So, you're not fired?"

"I'm not fired," he said. He smiled. "And I don't have to quit. Disclosure was what I needed to do and to remove myself from decisions about your career. And I did that. But…"

He stepped to her and put his hands around her waist. "We're not allowed to have any PDA at work. And we should, according to H.R., not make our relationship too obvious. At least, until we know what it is. So, make this kiss in your office count."

He leaned in and kissed her deeply. As he pulled back, she said quietly, "I was scared I might lose you."

"Me, too," he whispered.

Her phone going off broke the magic for a second. As she read the text a huge smile broke across her face. "Oh my God," she said.

"What?" he asked.

She gazed into his eyes with pure delight. "I got the Top Sail house."

"Holy shit, Summer, that's so fantastic," he said. He gave her waist a squeeze. "You can add to those wonderful memories now, huh?"

She nodded. "You'll help me make new ones?"

"You bet that sweet ass, I will," he said. She laughed as he gave her a little pat on the cheeks. As he started to pull away, she grabbed him, shut her office door, and pulled him into the corner.

"You know what, if we're going to make this kiss count," she said. "Then we're going to make it count."

They both laughed as they christened her office two times before lunch. And for the first time in a long time, she was truly happy.

12

What Happens Next?

"Holy—"

"Fucking—"

"Shit." Tabitha finished for Annie and Fawn.

"Summer, this is amazing," Fawn said. "Oh my God."

"Summer this is so great for you," Annie said quietly. "Love, huh?"

"I think it could be," Summer said. She took a sip of her drink as the waiter cleared their empty plates. "Can you believe it?"

"I can, yeah," Annie said.

Summer smiled at her green-eyed friend who knew her better than anyone.

"I think my mom would really like him," Summer said quietly.

"Oh, well then," Annie said. "We all have to meet him."

"Fuck to the yes," Tabitha said as she slapped the table. "We need to meet the Adonis who has won over our sultry Summer!"

"Absolutely," Fawn said.

"I want you all to meet him," Summer said. "But, maybe, not quite yet. Give me a little more time with him."

"I can't fucking believe his little brother was your first," Tabitha exclaimed.

They all laughed as Summer felt a blush cross her face. "My God, I know, right? Of all the guys our freshman year." She turned to face Annie with a shrug.

"I remember Damian," Annie said. "He was hot."

"He *was* hot," Fawn agreed.

"Fuck, I didn't get to meet him, I transferred in, remember?" Tabitha said.

"Our junior year," Summer said. "And none of us were ever the same after meeting you."

"You better fucking believe it," Tabitha exclaimed. She cheered them with her glass before taking a sip. She sat the glass down. "I need to see a pic. And don't tell me you didn't take a selfie with him, Summer, I know you."

"Picture time!" Annie exclaimed.

Summer pulled out her phone and the girls took turns ooo-ing and aww-ing over Ace as they passed her phone around. When it got back to Summer, she tucked it away with a smile.

"You look fucking happy," Tabitha said. "I fucking love this look on you."

"Me, too," Fawn said.

Summer smiled at them, then at Annie.

"So, what happens next?" Annie asked.

"I'm not sure," Summer said slowly. "And for the first time in my life, I'm totally okay with that."

"Would you consider marriage?" Fawn asked. "I've never thought you'd be up for it, but I'm thinking I was wrong about that."

Summer shrugged. "I guess I didn't consider it one way or the other," she said. "But now...I mean. Maybe, yeah."

"Well, I'm super happy for you," Annie said as she leaned back against her chair. "You deserve this. You really do. I can't wait to meet him."

"I can't wait for you to meet him, too," Summer said. "All of you."

"And we will be your first guests at the Top Sail house?" Tabitha asked.

Summer laughed as she took in all their warm stares.

"Of course," Summer said. She grabbed Annie's hand and squeezed. "You're my family. And there's no better place for family than Top Sail."

"Cheers to that," Fawn said.

They all raised their glasses in a noisy clink as Summer took a sip of her drink.

She couldn't wait to share this new part of her life with her friends. But especially, with Ace.

<u>**More to Come!**</u>

Summer's love story isn't over!
Keep reading the *Girls Who
Brunch Erotic Series* to see what
happens to Summer and Ace!
Wanna learn more about the other
ladies—Annie, Fawn, and Tabitha?
Keep reading the *Girls Who
Brunch Erotic Series* as they have
brunch, enjoy sex, and talk about it
all!

<u>**Review this book!**</u>

Do you love *Extra Whipped Cream*
as part of the *Girls Who Brunch
Erotic Series*? Then tell everyone
about it! Leave a review on
Amazon.com!

www.ingramcontent.com/pod-product-compliance
Lightning Source LLC
Chambersburg PA
CBHW031543310726
48971CB00008B/2602